Abner & Ian

GET RIGHT-SIDE UP

Story by **Dave Eggers**

Art by **Laura Park**

LB

Little, Brown and Company
New York Boston

Uh-oh.

What?

Can't you see? We're sideways.
We're supposed to be down *there*.
We can't start the story this way.

Oh. Right.

5

This is a problem.
What should we do?

Um. Did you have any ideas?
Usually you have such good ideas.

We can ask that kid for help.

That kid? I don't know.
There's a funny smell
coming from that direction.

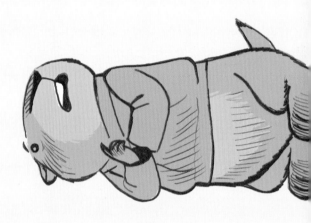

I don't smell anything.

I have a sensitive nose.

Hey, kid! We need a hand. Do us a favor.
Shake the book, then turn the page.

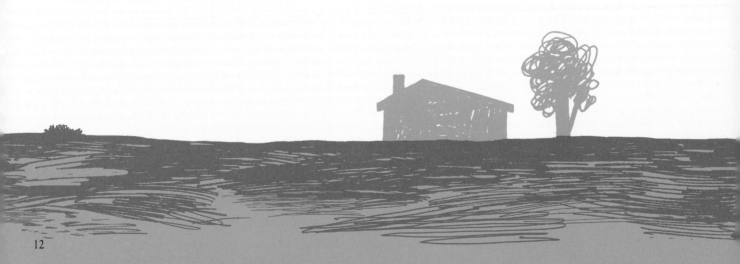

Wait. What? Why would
you want the kid to do *that*?

To get us right-side up. I've seen
it work before. Shake the book,
and when you turn the page,
everything's back in the right place.
Trust me. This is how it's done.

Oh. Okay. I think I heard that somewhere, too.

So, kid: When we say *Now*,
shake the book and turn the page.

Did you want *me* to say *Now*?

I was thinking I'd say it.
Did *you* want to say it?

If you don't mind.
I think I'd be really good at it.

Okay. Give it a try.
One.
Two.
Three.

This is exciting.

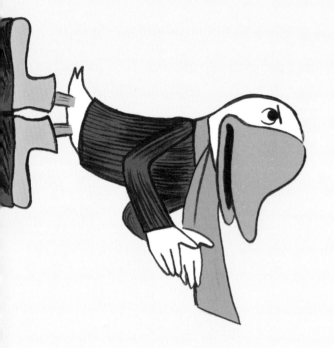

You're not supposed to say
This is exciting.
You're supposed to say *Now*!
Okay? So, are you ready?

I am so ready.
This is really a thrill.

Please stop describing how you feel about this. Do you know how long we've been perpendicular? My ankles are beginning to hurt. Now can we start?

Sure. But first do you think we should ask if the *kid* is ready?

The kid looks ready to me.
Kid, are you ready?

The kid said yes. Are you satisfied?

I am. I think reassurances like that are so helpful to the smooth functioning of systems, and greatly increase the probability of success in an endeavor like this.

Sigh. All right. Here we go.
After I say *One*, *two*, *three*, you say
Now! and the kid will shake the book
and turn the page.

One. Two. Three.

NOW!

Uh-oh. That didn't work at all.

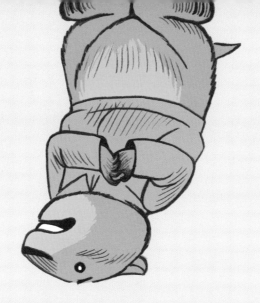

This is worse than before.
And I'm afraid of heights.

I didn't know that about you.

There are lots of things
you don't know about me.
I also have a brie allergy.
And recurrent eczema.

Normally I would be more fascinated by all that.
But we really need to get un–upside down.
Should we ask the kid again?

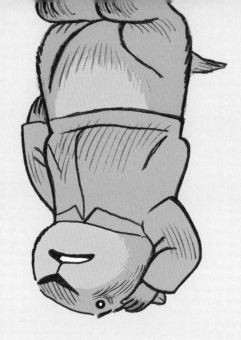

Yes. The blood is
rushing to my head.
And my elbows are numb.

Kid. On three, try it again. Shake the
book and turn the page. But do it harder
this time. One. Two. THREE!

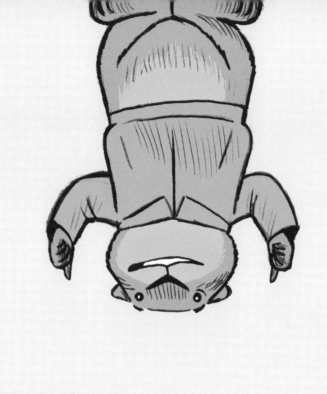

Whoa.

I did not see that coming.

Can you feel your tummy?

I'm not sure.
It might be *your* tummy I'm feeling.
Can you feel *my* tummy?

You know what? I'm getting the feeling this kid doesn't have the touch. Kid, is there anyone nearby who can help? A parent? Maybe a pet with opposable thumbs?

I think the kid is okay.
Kid, you're okay.

Fine. Let's try it again. This time
even harder and crazier, okay, kid?
One. Two. THREE!

Hm. At least we're right-side up.

Yes, but I feel like all that stuff above us—
like, everything on Earth—could fall on our heads.

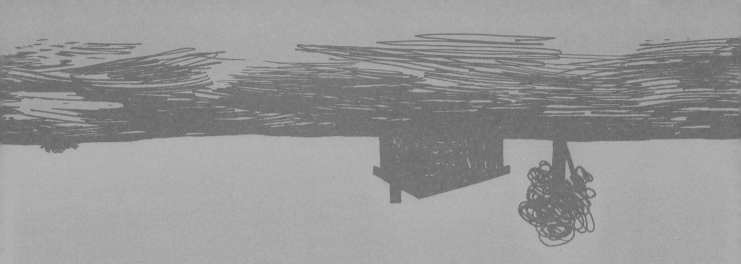

You want to risk it again?

I don't see how it can get any worse.

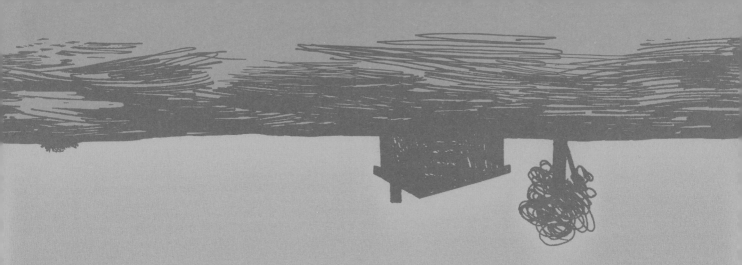

Okay. Kid. Shake and turn the page.
Crazier than ever before. Now!

I'm beginning to think this kid is doing this on purpose.

I don't think the kid is doing it
on purpose. I actually think—

Let's just keep trying till we get it right.
Quickly and cuckoo-crazy, kid.
Shake and turn!

Um...

Nope. Again!

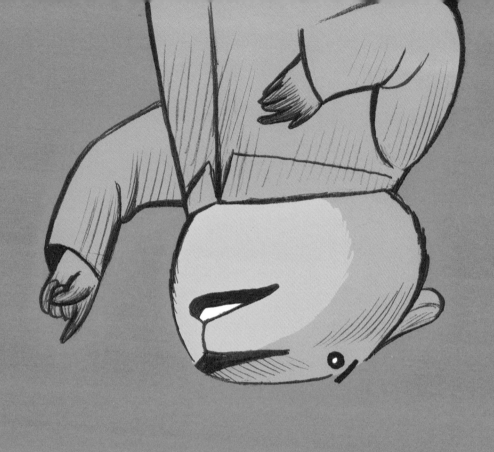

Excuse me…

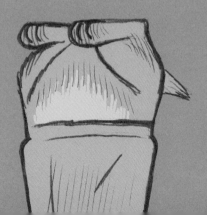

Again! Like a gorilla!

Hm.

I'm kind of thinking we just need to rest a second.

Rest a second?
When we're so close?
Kid, let's go one more time!
Shake and turn!

This looks familiar.

Please. I think we need to pause.
What if we just *waited*?

Just *waited*? Wait for what?

Wait for things to settle. We keep telling the kid to shake and turn, and nothing's getting better. The harder the kid shakes, the weirder things become. What if we just waited a second? Or even *ten* seconds? We can't fight madness with madness and hope to find sanity.

I don't see how—

Shhh. Relax.

Kid? Can you turn out the
light and count to ten?
Take it slow. We'll meet you
on page 76.

One...   Two...

Three...   Four...   Five...

Six...   Seven...   Eight...

Nine...   Ten.

Wow. You were right, Ian. We're right-side up!

I have a good idea every now and then, too, Abner.
So, are we finally ready to start the story?

What? After all that, I'm ready for a nap.
Kid, turn the book on its side so I can lie down.

No. Nope. No.
Kid, do not do what the duck says.
When I count to three and say *Now*,
just close the book. It'll be nice and dark
and the duck can sleep a happy sleep.
One.
Two.
Three.

Now.

The illustrations for this book were drawn with pencil and colored with a computer. This book was edited by Andrea Spooner and designed by Dave Eggers with art direction by Dave Caplan. The production was supervised by Ruiko Tokunaga, and the production editor was Jen Graham. The text was set in Fournier.

• Little, Brown and Company • Hachette Book Group • 1290 Avenue of the Americas, New York, NY 10104 • Visit us at LBYR.com • First Edition: May 2019 • Little, Brown and Company is a division of Hachette Book Group, Inc. • The Little, Brown name and logo are trademarks of Hachette Book Group, Inc. • The publisher is not responsible for websites (or their content) that are not owned by the publisher. • Library of Congress Cataloging-in-Publication Data • Names: Eggers, Dave, author. | Park, Laura, 1980- illustrator. • Title: Abner & Ian get right-side up / story by Dave Eggers ; illustrated by Laura Park. • Description: First edition. | New York ; Boston : LB keys/Little, Brown and Company, 2019. | Summary: Abner the duck and Ian the prairie dog are stuck sideways on the book's pages, and they will need the reader's help to set things right for storytime. • Identifiers: LCCN 2018022801| ISBN 9780316485869 (hardcover) | ISBN 9780316485838 (ebook) | ISBN 9780316485852 (library edition ebook) • Subjects: | CYAC: Books and reading— Fiction. | Ducks—Fiction. | Prairie dogs—Fiction. | Humorous stories. • Classification: LCC PZ7.1.E296 Abn 2019 | DDC [E]—dc23 • LC record available at https://lccn.loc.gov/2018022801 • ISBNs: 978-0-316-48586-9 (hardcover), 978-0-316-48583-8 (ebook), 978-0-316-48584-5 (ebook), 978-0-316-48577-7 (ebook) • PRINTED IN CHINA • 1010 • 10 9 8 7 6 5 4 3 2 1